BIFF! BANG! POW!

Sandra Quan D'Eramo

Editorial Board

Jennifer Glass • Kathleen Gould Lundy • Joan Green

ACKNOWLEDGMENTS

The publisher gratefully acknowledges the following for permission to reprint copyrighted material in this book.

"Stan Lee, Truly an Icon" by Andrew Kardon, *Wired Magazine,* October 26, 2009. Copyright © 2009 Condé Nast Publications. All rights reserved. Originally published in Wired.com. Reprinted by permission. Found at http://www.wired.com/geekdad/2009/10/stan-lee-truly-an-icon/

Every reasonable effort has been made to trace the owners of copyrighted material and to make due acknowledgment. Any errors or omissions drawn to our attention will be gladly rectified in future editions.

Photo Credits: Page 18: *Fantastic Four*–Photo by UNIMEDIA IMAGES/ ADC/KEYSTONE Press © Copyright 2007 by ADC; Page 19: *Peace Party*– © Copyright 1999 Blue Corn Comics. All rights reserved; *X Men*–TM & © 2010 Marvel Entertainment LLC and its subsidiaries. Used with permission; Page 20: *League of Extraordinary Gentlemen*–© 2003 20th Century Fox; *THE 99*–Courtesy of Teshkeel Media Group; Page 21: *Naruto*–© Copyright 1999 by Masashi Kishimoto/SHUEISHA Inc.; Page 22: *AK Comics*–KHALED DESOUKI/AFP/Getty Images; *Al Gough*–©ZUMAPRESS.com/Keystone Press; Page 23: *Grant Morrison*–Photo by pinguino/public domain; Page 32: *Stan Lee*–Photo by Frank Micelotta/Getty Images for Spike TV; All other images–Shutterstock, iStockphoto.

HOUGHTON MIFFLIN HARCOURT

10801 N. Mopac Expressway
Building # 3
Austin, TX 78759
1.800.531.5015

Steck-Vaughn is a trademark of HMH Supplemental Publishers Inc. registered in the United States of America and/or other jurisdictions. All inquiries should be mailed to HMH Supplemental Publishers Inc., P.O. Box 27010, Austin, TX 78755.

Ru'bĭcon
www.rubiconpublishing.com

Associate Publisher: Kim Koh
Editorial Director: Amy Land
Editor: Joyce Thian
Creative Director: Jennifer Drew
Art Director: Jen Harvey
Graphic Designer: Jason Mitchell
Cover Image: iStockphoto.com

Printed in Singapore

ISBN: 978-1-77058-419-8
2 3 4 5 6 7 8 9 10 11   2016   23 22 21 20 19 18 17 16 15 14
A B C D E F G

SEE
What do you see in this picture?

THINK
What do you think is happening in this picture?

TALK
With a partner, brainstorm a list of words that describe what you see in this picture.

DO
With a partner, create a title for this picture. You might want to use some of the words you discussed.

AKIO'S AMAZING COMIC

Illustrated by Jim Jimenez

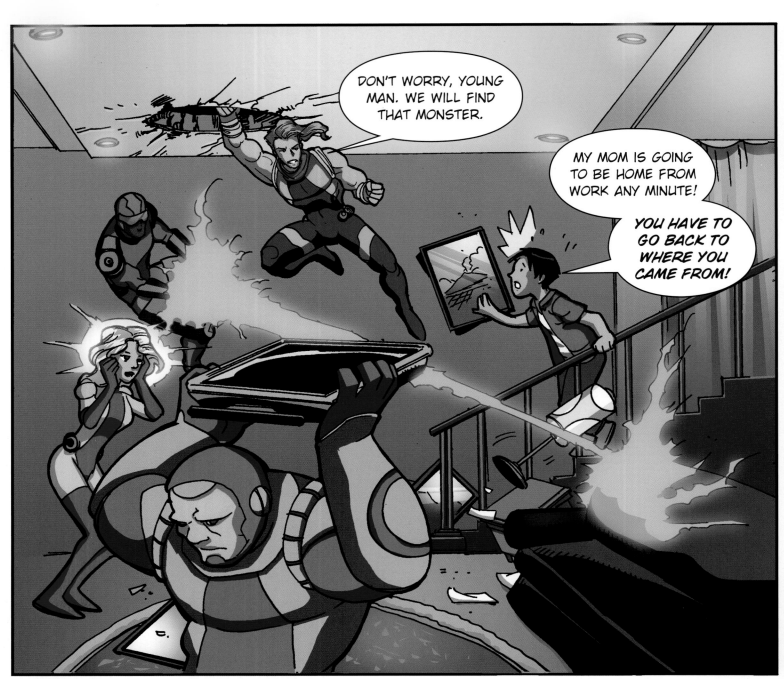

AKIO QUICKLY READS THE SECOND HALF OF THE RHYME.

GO BACK, BACK, BACK TO WHERE YOU BELONG. AND MAKE EVERYTHING AS IT WAS ALL ALONG.

SEE YOU LATER, KID!

FOOOOOSSHH!

I'M HOME!

WHEW! JUST IN TIME.

HEY, KIDDO.

HOW ABOUT SEEING THAT SUPERHERO MOVIE TONIGHT?

SPEAK OUT With a partner, discuss a time when you have narrowly avoided getting into trouble for breaking something at home or making a mess. After your discussion, evaluate your own performance.

COMIC-BOOK BREAKDOWN

PANELS

Each panel captures a scene. Panels can be different shapes and sizes. Sometimes, a panel might even fill an entire page.

CAPTIONS

Captions add information that is not obvious from the art or the text. Captions are usually placed at the top of the panels and are read first.

ACTION LINES

Action lines are drawn beside people or objects to show that they're moving.

SPEECH BALLOONS

Speech balloons contain what a character is saying. They usually look like smooth bubbles. A speech balloon with jagged edges might mean that a character is shouting or speaking through some sort of device, such as a telephone.

SPEAK UP With a partner, talk about why you think comic books are so popular. Why do people of all ages read them?

HIGH ABOVE THE CITY HE HAS SWORN TO PROTECT, THE RUBY BATTLES THE FORCES OF NATURE.

I CAN'T LET THE PEOP OF MAJOR CIT DOWN!

BOOM!

KRA-KOOM!

DOWN TO MY LAST OUNCE OF STRENGTH ...

SKY FALLS SILENT. PASSED!

FINALLY. IT'S OVER.

BUT NOT EVERYONE DELIGHTS IN OUR HERO'S VICTORY.

CELEBRATE TODAY, CITIZENS OF MAJOR CITY. TOMORROW YOU WILL KNEEL BEFORE TOCKS!

HURRAY! RUBY! THE

TO BE CONTINUED ...

THOUGHT BALLOONS

Thought balloons contain what a character is thinking. They look like clouds.

POINTERS

Pointers are the tails of speech and thought balloons. They show which character is speaking or thinking.

GUTTER

The gutter is the space that separates the panels.

SOUND EFFECTS

Sound effects are stylized sound words. They represent actions or noises within a scene.

FRAMES

Frames are the borders around panels. If a panel shows a dream or an imaginary scene, its frame might be wavy or look like the edges of a cloud.

TALK TIP

When you are giving someone feedback, be specific. Say exactly what you like about the person's work and explain why you like it. If you think there is something that needs improvement, suggest ways that it could be fixed.

SPEAK OUT

With a partner, write a brief skit for a conversation between two comic book fans. Be sure to use terms from the selection in your skit. Practice and perform your skit for another pair of students. Evaluate your own performance.

BOOM!
SOUND EFFECTS 101

SPEAK UP

Working with a partner, make a list of sound effects that could be used in any style or genre of comic book.

Q: What's so special about sound effects in comic books?

A: They can help tell the story. For example, an "AH-CHOO!" effectively shows that a character is sneezing. Without it, his or her silent twisted face might just confuse readers. Writers can also use sound effects to increase the action and drama of a scene.

AHH-CHOOO!

SLAM!

Q: What makes a good sound effect?

A: To be believable, a sound effect has to — duh! — sound like the action or object it's meant to represent. This is called onomatopoeia (aw-nuh-mah-tuh-pea-uh).

TALK TIP

When you come to a difficult word, try sounding it out, or work with a partner or teacher to figure out the pronunciation. The dictionary is also a good place to go to for help.

Q: When shouldn't sound effects be used?

A: Scott Allie, an editor and writer for Dark Horse Comics, says: "My rule of thumb is to only use them if they aid storytelling. I don't need to 'hear' a faucet running if I'm given a close-up of the faucet running. ... I [also] don't really need to hear a punch, unless I'm supposed to know that it's a really strong punch."

 **Q:** Who comes up with sound effects?

 A: Usually, it is the writer who comes up with the original sound effect.

 Q: Who actually puts the sound effects into a comic book?

 A: A letterer draws the sound word into a scene, either by hand or on the computer.

 Q: What happens when comic-book creators invent a specific sound effect for their characters?

 A: They sometimes trademark their creations. For example, Marvel owns "THWIP!" (the sound of Spider-Man's web shooter) and "SNIKT!" (the switchblade-like sound of Wolverine's claws locking into place).

---

trademark: legally reserved for use only by the owner

Most comic-book readers are familiar with common sound effects like "BUZZ" (flying bees) or "HISS" (a slithering snake). Then there are effects like "BALLOOM!" that sound interesting but leave most readers puzzled. Try to match these creative sound effects to the actions or objects they were meant to represent:

SFX

- BALLOOM!
- CLANK!
- FWHEEEEE!
- GGLLAGGGG
- KA-ROOOOOSH!
- PWAKA-PWOOM!
- ZOOOSHHH!
- VRZM!
- THRAKAKA KAKAKAKA!
- SRAAK!

THE SOUND OF ...

- ☐ GURGLING
- ☐ AN OBJECT MOVING OR EXPANDING AT GREAT SPEED
- ☐ SOMETHING SUDDENLY COMING INTO EXISTENCE IN THIS DIMENSION
- ☐ ENERGY BOLTS
- ☐ A SPEEDING VEHICLE COLLIDING WITH OTHER VEHICLES
- ☐ AIR ESCAPING FROM A BALLOON
- ☐ METALLIC OR MECHANICAL BANGING
- ☑ A VOLCANO BEGINNING TO ERUPT
- ☐ BREAKING CONCRETE
- ☐ AN EXPLOSION

WERE YOU STUMPED, OR DID YOU GET THEM ALL? FIND THE ANSWERS ON PAGE 48!

WAIT! THERE'S MORE!

Did you know? DC Comics has a super villain called Onomatopoeia. He first appeared in March 2002. He got his nickname because he imitates the noises around him, such as dripping taps and gunshots. A comic-book critic called him "one of the coolest new villains of the decade."

SCREEEAAAAWRRR!

SPEAK OUT

With a partner, perform the selection as a read-aloud for another pair of students. Evaluate your own performance.

TALK TIP

Practice adjusting your voice in different ways for different effects. Choosing the right volume, tone, and emphasis helps you get your message across to your listeners.

COMIC SPEAK

SPEAK UP

With other members of a small group, share your favorite sayings from comic books or movies based on comic books. Talk about what makes these sayings effective.

Comic books are fun to read because they use everyday language, slang, and idioms. Action heroes especially like to use idioms, or phrases that mean more than their words put together. Idioms are colorful and lively expressions — perfect for comic heroes! Here are just a few of the most common idioms often found in comic books ...

ALL IN A DAY'S WORK

Expected and normal
"DEFEAT THE BAD GUY AND SAVE THE WORLD — ALL IN A DAY'S WORK."

BRING IT ON

Begin a fight or competition
"WE'VE ALREADY PREPARED FOR THE WORST, SO BRING IT ON."

GET AWAY WITH

Escape blame or punishment for something
"YOU WON'T GET AWAY WITH THIS, YOU VILE VILLAIN."

GO THROUGH SOMEONE

Fight or make it past someone to get to another

"NOT SO FAST. IF YOU WANT HIM, YOU'LL HAVE TO GO THROUGH ALL OF US FIRST."

WIPE THE FLOOR WITH

Defeat easily; overwhelm

"YOU'RE MESSING WITH THE WRONG PERSON. SHE'S GOING TO WIPE THE FLOOR WITH YOU!"

OVER MY DEAD BODY

In no way; under no circumstances

"THEY'RE PLANNING TO STEAL OUR POWER RINGS? OVER MY DEAD BODY!"

TALK TIP

The more you know about your topic and the more you prepare, the less nervous you will be when making a presentation. It also helps to take a deep breath right before you start.

SPEAK OUT

With other members of a small group, discuss the idioms, slang expressions, and sayings from the selection. Would you ever use any of these in your own everyday speech? Following the discussion, evaluate your own performance.

SUPERHERO DREAM TEAMS

SPEAK UP

With other members of a small group, talk about the advantages of working in a team. In what situations would working in a team be better than working on your own?

Comic-book creators know that even superheroes with super powers need a helping hand sometimes. And when superheroes work in teams, there's nothing that can stop them! Here is a small selection of superhero teams that work together to make the world a safer place ...

Fantastic Four

First appeared in:
Fantastic Four (1961)

Made up of:
Human Torch, the Thing, Invisible Woman, and Mister Fantastic

What's their story?
These four superhuman champions are internationally famous. They fight evil super villains and try to make the world a better place through scientific discovery.

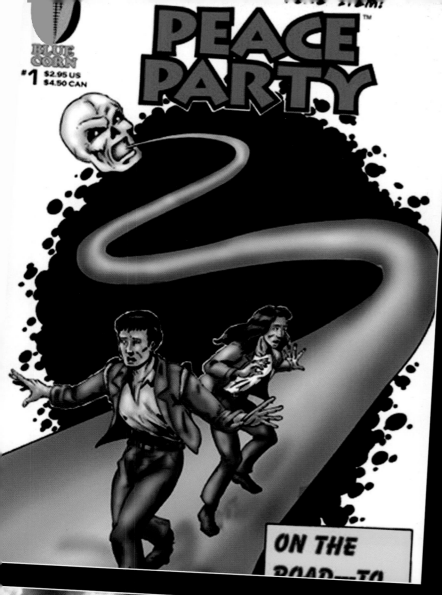

Peace Party

First appeared in:
Peace Party (2001)

Made up of:
Rain Falling and Snake Standing

What's their story?
This superhero duo was granted super powers by a mystical being. As defenders of the world, they must fight everything from prejudice and pollution to super villains and the supernatural. They always try to find a peaceful solution to these problems.

X-Men

First appeared in:
X-Men (1963)

Made up of:
Cyclops, Iceman, Angel, Beast, and Marvel Girl originally, but the group has changed over time as more mutants have joined and others have left

What's their story?
Led by Professor Xavier, the X-Men protect humankind from mutants who want to take over the world. The X-Men try to show the world that mutants can be good, too. They got their name because they each have an "extra" ability that normal humans don't have.

The League of Extraordinary Gentlemen

First appeared in:
The League of Extraordinary Gentlemen (1999)

Made up of:
Allan Quartermain, Captain Nemo, Dr. Jekyll (and Mr. Hyde), the Invisible Man, Dorian Gray, Mina Harker, and Tom Sawyer

What's their story?
It is the year 1899. The British Empire is under great threat. To protect the empire, a secret organization forms a league of extraordinary individuals with extraordinary abilities.

The 99

First appeared in:
The 99: Origins (2006)

Made up of:
From Noora "The Truth Seer" to Jami "The Assembler," this team boasts 99 unique superheroes, each with a different quality

What's their story?
A group of ordinary people develop amazing abilities after coming into contact with mystical gems infused with power and wisdom. Together they battle injustice and try to make the world right again.

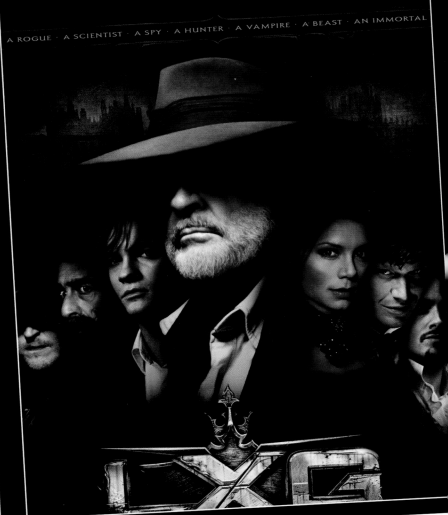

Team Kakashi

First appeared in:
Naruto (1999)

Made up of:
Naruto, Sakura, Sasuke, and their leader (or sensei) Kakashi

What's their story?
Team Kakashi must complete various missions on behalf of its village of Konoha. But there are dangers everywhere, including enemies from other villages. These four skilled ninjas must work together if they want to succeed — and make it back home alive.

Who is your hero? Prepare a brief oral narrative telling the story of the person you consider your hero. Perform your narrative for a partner. Evaluate your own performance.

LISTEN UP

While listening to someone make a presentation, take notes to help keep track of or summarize important points.

Let's Hear It for SUPERHEROES

SPEAK UP
With a partner, make a list of all the comic-book superheroes you know of. Which do you like the most and why?

Comic-book superheroes — meaningful or meaningless? Find out what these comic-book creators have to say. Then, decide for yourself!

"I BELIEVE THAT HAVING SUPERHEROES, OR SUPERHUMAN BEINGS, IS AN ESSENTIAL NEED. ... WE NEED TO BELIEVE IN A HIGHER BEING THAT WILL BE THERE FOR HELP, AND CAN EFFECT CHANGE ON HIS OWN."

— Marwan Nashar, managing editor of AK Comics

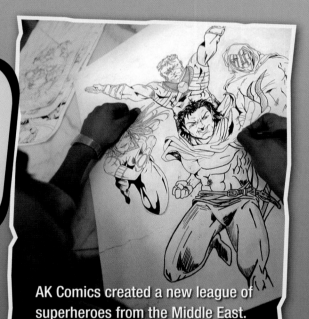

AK Comics created a new league of superheroes from the Middle East.

"I THINK [SUPERHEROES] REPRESENT THE BEST OF OURSELVES AND THE PEOPLE WE'D LIKE TO BE. THEN ALSO, I THINK THERE IS THE *WISH FULFILLMENT* THAT YOU CAN SOMETIMES FEEL POWERLESS IN THE WORLD AND, IF YOU HAD THESE ABILITIES, YOU COULD FIGHT BACK."

— Al Gough, co-writer of the movie script for *Spider-Man 2*

WISH FULFILLMENT: achieving something that you want in real life in an imaginary situation, such as a dream, movie, book, etc.

"A GOOD COMIC-BOOK SUPERHERO STORY, LIKE ANY GOOD STORY, SATISFIES OUR NEED TO ESCAPE."
— David Gabriel, executive director of the New York City Comic Book Museum

"SUPERHERO COMICS CAN DO THINGS THAT THE REAL WORLD CAN'T DO. THAT'S WHY PEOPLE LIKE THEM. THAT'S WHY WE ENJOY THEM AS AN ESCAPE. THEY CAN TAKE US TO PLACES THE REAL WORLD CAN'T. THE REAL WORLD IS CRUEL, BUT SUPERHERO COMICS ARE FANTASTIC."
— Grant Morrison, comic-book writer

"HEROES BORE ME. SUPERHEROES, THEREFORE, SUPERBORE ME. ... BECAUSE THEIR HEROISM PAINTS THEM INTO A CORNER ... IT *DEPRIVES* THE CHARACTERS OF THE RIGHT TO BE HUMAN."
— Barb Cooper, co-creator of the graphic novel *Half Dead*

DEPRIVES: denies; takes away

"IF SOME PEOPLE ARE BORED WITH THE SUPERHERO, MAYBE IT'S BECAUSE THE CREATORS ARE BORED THEMSELVES AND THEREFORE ARE CREATING BORING SUPERHERO STORIES."
— Vince Moore, editor for DarkStorm Studios

LISTEN UP

When you listen to a presentation, make eye contact with the presenter, sit up straight, and give the presenter your full attention. This will help the speaker relax and give a more effective performance.

SPEAK OUT

Have you ever wished that you had super powers like a superhero? Did you ever pretend to be a superhero when you were little? Prepare a brief oral narrative in which you tell a story about a time you pretended that you had super powers. Perform your narrative for a partner. Have your partner evaluate your performance and provide feedback.

MANGA Minute

SPEAK UP With other members of a small group, discuss manga. How many group members like this form of comic? What do members like or dislike about it?

LISTEN UP

Listen politely to the opinions of others, even if they differ from your own. Then you are more likely to be shown the same respect.

I HEART MANGA

SEARCH

MANGA

poindexter82 | 24 November
Subscribe to this Discussion
Topics: manga, comics, Japan

I have heard a lot about manga. Everyone is talking about them at school. I'm thinking of picking one up at the library. What should I know before I begin?

Reply

GregInTheMachine86 | 24 November
Ohaiyo! If you want to know more about manga, then you've come to the right place. We're all huge fans of manga here. For starters, manga (pronounced mawn-gah) are basically Japanese comic books.

Reply

LadyManga | 24 November
They're a pretty big deal in Japan. Almost everyone there reads manga. Billions of copies of manga books and magazines are sold every year.
Reply

SamIAm | 24 November
Yes, people of all ages in Japan read manga. There are special terms for different kinds of manga:
    Shonen (show-nen) is for boys
    Shojo (show-joe) is for girls
    Seinen (say-nen) is for men
    Josei (joe-say) is for women
    Kodomo (koh-doe-moe) is for young kids
Reply

999KD | 24 November
Here's an important tip: Manga are read from right to left, following traditional Japanese writing. Some publishers who print manga books for English audiences will flip the pages to change the reading direction to left to right. They do this because they think people are more used to reading left to right. Many people, however, don't like the practice of "flipping" because they believe it often leads to really bad errors.
Reply

poindexter82 | 24 November
Bad errors? Like what?
Reply

25

999KD | 25 November

Well, for example, flipping an image of a handshake will make it look as if the characters are shaking with their left hands. That looks strange, but it's not the worst example of a bad flip. Think of how confusing it would be if an image of a clock were flipped. If its hands originally pointed to 3 o'clock, it would suddenly point to 9 o'clock. Oh, and a nametag that used to say "TOM" would read "MOT" when flipped!

Reply

123445uss | 26 November

I'm learning the manga style of drawing right now, and here's what I know so far: A lot of manga characters are drawn with large round eyes. This style started with Osamu Tezuka (Oss-ah-moo Tezz-oo-kah). He's a really famous *mangaka* (mawn-gah-kah), or comic author/artist.

Reply

CioCioSan | 26 November

Osamu Tezuka is a legend! Many people call him the "father of manga." He sold some 100 million books in his lifetime. He created the super popular *Astro Boy*. Tezuka died at the age of 60 in 1989.

Reply

Kai10342 | 28 November

Generally, manga books are much thicker than North American single comics. Running anywhere from 150 to 350 pages, manga are designed to be speed-read — you need only three to four seconds to read each page.

Reply

GregInTheMachine86 | 29 November

Manga stories often run longer than Western comics because they tend to move a lot slower. For example, a single sword fight can last over 30 pages from beginning to end.

Reply

poindexter82 | 30 November

Cool, thanks for all your responses, everyone. I can't wait to read my first manga!

Reply

Add Your Comment | Login to Leave a Message

Related Discussions

Japanese manga versus American comics

10 replies | 13 Feb

Anime based on manga

32 replies | 21 Mar

Tips on drawing manga style of art

13 replies | 30 Dec

Must-read manga

13 replies | 5 Jun

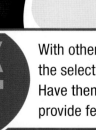

TALK TIP

When performing a read-aloud, listen carefully to the sections read by others. This will help you read with the appropriate volume and expression.

SPEAK OUT

With other members of a small group, perform the selection as a read-aloud for another group. Have them evaluate your performance and provide feedback.

SPEAK UP Have you ever thought about what you want to do when you are older? Share your goals with other members of a small group.

You love reading, collecting, and learning about comics. Have you ever thought about working with comic books? Take this short survey to find out how and where you could use your talents!

1 The subject I like the most at school is …

a) Language Arts
b) Art
c) Everything — I like every subject that I study
d) Math

2 I like tasks where I get to …

a) Come up with new ideas
b) Design things
c) Solve problems
d) Work with others

3 My classmates would say that I am …

a) Imaginative
b) Creative
c) Logical
d) Outgoing

4 My teachers would say that I am …

a) Inventive
b) Artistic
c) Organized
d) Energetic

AT JOB!

5 When I am talking with others …

a) I explain my ideas well
b) I am a good listener
c) I like to share my point of view
d) I am usually pretty animated

---

6 When I am working in a group, I usually …

a) Come up with the most ideas
b) Can visualize what everyone is saying
c) Am the leader or organizer
d) Am most comfortable presenting the final product on behalf of my group

---

7 When I am assigned an independent study project …

a) I am most excited about being able to choose what I want to do
b) I always include my own artwork and put together the final draft with care
c) I like to help my classmates double-check their work
d) I most enjoy presenting my project to the class

---

8 If my class was going to raise money for a good cause, I would help with …

a) Writing fundraising letters
b) Drawing or designing posters, banners, or flyers
c) Organizing and making sure that everything runs smoothly
d) Promoting the event

Look at your answers. See which letter appears the most.

MOSTLY A

The write stuff! If you answered mostly A, you could be a writer. A comic-book writer comes up with ideas for new stories, characters, and even entire imaginary universes. He or she prepares the script, including the dialogue, captions, and scene directions to tell artists what to draw.

MOSTLY B

Drawing from experience! If you answered mostly B, you might enjoy doing the artwork in a comic book. First, an illustrator draws the art for a comic book in black and white. The illustrator usually uses a pencil. Next, an inker goes over the pencil lines with ink to make them stand out. Then, a colorist adds the color to the drawings. Finally, a letterer adds the text and sound effects to the art.

MOSTLY C

Team captain! If you answered mostly C, you would make a good editor. An editor works with the entire team to make sure the comic book is a good creative product, is finished on time, and has no mistakes in it.

MOSTLY D

That's hype! If you answered mostly D, you might like marketing comic books. A marketer tries to get more readers interested in a comic book. This might mean putting out advertising, organizing promotional events, building a website, or getting a booth at comic-book conventions. A marketer might even come up with ideas for related merchandise, such as video games and movies.

TALK TIP

When performing a skit, you may read your lines from a script. However, you should still try to use appropriate facial expressions to make your character come to life.

SPEAK OUT

With a partner, write a brief skit of a conversation between two people working in the comic book industry. Include information from the selection in your skit. Practice and perform your skit for another pair of students. Have them evaluate your performance and provide feedback.

Stan Lee, Truly an Icon

Wired Magazine, October 26, 2009

By Andrew Kardon

SPEAK UP Tell a partner about a person that you really admire. Why does this person inspire you? Describe one thing that this person has said or done to impress you.

Y ou don't have to be a true believer to know the name Stan Lee. The co-creator of such popular superheroes as Spider-Man, Iron Man, and Hulk, Stan "The Man" Lee helped make Marvel Comics the company it is today. In short, he's an industry icon. ...

GEEKDAD: You were just honored with a Comic-Con Icon Award at the "Scream 2009" Show … What does this Icon Award mean to you?

Stan Lee: Well, it means I have to find some more room on my shelf I guess. No, it's wonderful, because it's an award that's given by the fans and that always means so much. When you're in entertainment, the fans are everything. If the fans relate to you, like your work, then you have succeeded, no matter what. Apparently, the fans were very excited about all of the people that were there. Including me. So it was a very gratifying evening.

GD: Kids are always looking up to heroes. So how do you think the heroes which you helped create — like Spider-Man, Hulk, and the Fantastic Four — affect kids today?

SL: Apparently, from what I've been told over the years by fans, they've meant a lot to them. I've had people come up to me and say that they had unhappy childhoods and reading these stories was the one glow, the one happy thing that would happen to them. And I seem to remember when I was a kid, when I was young and unhappy, I'd pick up a copy of the *Hardy Boys* or a Jules Verne story and that would make me feel good. So I can relate to that. And I was so happy that people would put the stories that I had written in the same area as the things that had made me happy when I was a kid.

---

gratifying: pleasing; satisfying

GD: Do you remember what the first comic book was that you read as a kid?

SL: No I don't. I never knew I'd be interviewed about it later. In those days, when I was a kid, the comic books were mostly reprints of newspaper strips. So I'd be reading *Flash Gordon* or *Dick Tracy* or *Little Orphan Annie* taken from the newspapers. I think the first two that were original that I read were *Superman* and then *Captain America*. I liked both of those.

GD: What do you think about the future of comics? With digital comics and online comics starting to take hold, will we see the end of comics in print?

SL: Years ago, people thought that nobody would buy books anymore when television came along, but the book business is still good. I hope that comic books in their present form will always remain. There'll be graphic novels. They'll be on better paper, but still, you can carry them with you, you can fold them and put them in your pocket so to speak. You can share them with a friend. You can collect them. And you can reread them and they're fun and they're pleasant. It's just like a newspaper. I love reading a newspaper. I hope that computers never are the death knell of newspapers because there's something about reading a newspaper — holding it in your hand and turning the pages — that nothing can replace. So I'm hoping comics will hang around. ...

death knell: something that ushers in the end or destruction

GD: What's your advice to any kids out there who want to be comic writers someday?

SL: To be a comic-book writer is harder and harder. It used to be that you can write comics even though you might not have been able to write anything else because they weren't that particular. If a guy could just put a couple of panels together, he could write a comic. But today some of the best writers in America are writing comics. Just as some of the best artists are now drawing them. And we have screenwriters and television writers and novelists who are doing comics now. So the best way to become a comic-book writer is first become a really, really good writer. Not a comic-book writer, but a good writer. And once you've mastered the art of simply doing creative writing, then you start concentrating on comics. But you can't come in to the field unless you start out by being a really good writer.

GD: Out of all the super powers you could possibly have, which one would you want?

SL: Believe it or not, good luck. Because if you're lucky then everything goes right for you. Right? If somebody shoots at you, they'll miss. Somebody takes a swing at you, they'll trip and fall before the blow lands. If you buy a lottery ticket, you're sure to win. I think luck is really the most important thing you could have.

TALK TIP _____

When practicing for a read-aloud, be sure to learn the pronunciation and meaning of any unfamiliar words.

SPEAK OUT

With a partner, practice and perform the selection as a read-aloud for another pair of students. Have them evaluate your performance and provide feedback.

THE SPECIAL EDITION

Illustrated by Robert Deas

SPEAK UP

With other members of a small group, list the different things that people like to collect, such as comic books. Why is collecting such a popular hobby?

Evan jumped out of bed. He was so excited. Today was the day. He and his friends had been talking about this for months. Evan had even bought a calendar and crossed off each day as it passed.

After months of waiting, the Richmond Comic-Con had finally arrived!

Evan had gone to other comic-book conventions before. But this one was special. Extra special. The great Isaiah Jarrell was going to be there in person, signing autographs! Evan loved his comic book, *The Great Birdman*. It was the best comic in the whole wide world. A special collector's edition issue was being sold at the convention, and Jarrell was autographing each copy.

"Dad! I'm ready! Let's go! I don't want to be late!" Evan yelled as he ran down the stairs.

Evan's dad laughed. "Someone sounds excited. Well, we still have half an hour before we need to leave the house. Here, have some breakfast first."

"Oh, and um … can I have $30 for the new *Great Birdman* comic book?" Evan asked.

"Did you say $30? That's a pretty penny!"

"But, Dad, it's a special edition! And I need it to get Isaiah Jarrell's autograph!"

"I'm sorry, Evan, but that is just too much money. We can't afford $30 right now."

Evan's heart sank. He didn't want to make his dad feel bad, but he really wanted the comic book.

LISTEN UP

People are communicating at all times — even if they aren't speaking. They might be "saying" something with eye contact, facial expressions, or body language.

Evan was so preoccupied with thoughts of not being able to get his idol's autograph that he didn't even notice his dad leaving the kitchen. When Evan looked up, his dad was already gone. Evan stuck his head into the dining room and downstairs office but didn't see his dad anywhere.

Evan began to worry. Maybe he had hurt his dad's feelings. Then he heard the familiar click of his dad's cane coming up from the basement. In his dad's hand was an old comic book.

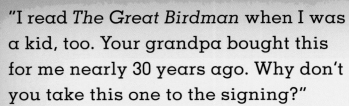

"I read *The Great Birdman* when I was a kid, too. Your grandpa bought this for me nearly 30 years ago. Why don't you take this one to the signing?"

Evan looked at the comic book. It was still in pretty good condition, but it had completely yellowed with age. And the pictures looked so old. The Great Birdman was even wearing a different costume.

Evan looked at his dad's face. He seemed so happy to give Evan his old comic book. Evan didn't want to hurt his dad's feelings.

"Thanks, Dad. I love it." Evan said. He tucked the old comic book in his jacket and gave his dad a hug.

Evan's friends were already waiting outside the convention center when he and his dad arrived. They were talking excitedly about the special edition of *The Great Birdman*. They all had their money ready to buy their copies. Evan didn't mention the old issue he had brought and neither did his dad. Evan just smiled and let his friends talk.

Once they got inside, they joined the line for the Isaiah Jarrell autograph signing session. It was a long wait but it was worth it. When it was finally their turn, Evan let his friends go first. They walked up one by one, paid for their special edition comic books, and took photos with Isaiah Jarrell as he signed their copies. They were all so excited and happy. No one noticed Evan's long face as he went up to the table.

Evan looked at his idol and said, "Sir, I don't have enough money to buy the new comic book. Could you sign my dad's old issue instead? It would make him really happy."

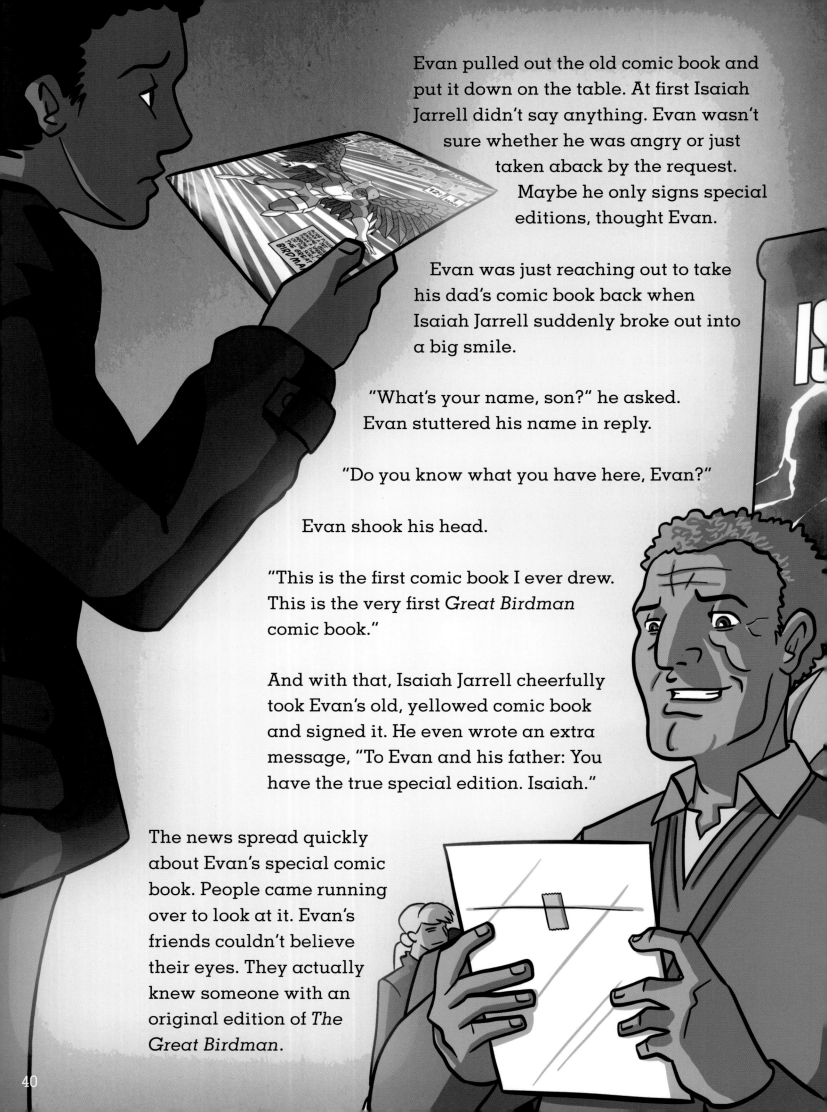

Evan pulled out the old comic book and put it down on the table. At first Isaiah Jarrell didn't say anything. Evan wasn't sure whether he was angry or just taken aback by the request. Maybe he only signs special editions, thought Evan.

Evan was just reaching out to take his dad's comic book back when Isaiah Jarrell suddenly broke out into a big smile.

"What's your name, son?" he asked. Evan stuttered his name in reply.

"Do you know what you have here, Evan?"

Evan shook his head.

"This is the first comic book I ever drew. This is the very first *Great Birdman* comic book."

And with that, Isaiah Jarrell cheerfully took Evan's old, yellowed comic book and signed it. He even wrote an extra message, "To Evan and his father: You have the true special edition. Isaiah."

The news spread quickly about Evan's special comic book. People came running over to look at it. Evan's friends couldn't believe their eyes. They actually knew someone with an original edition of *The Great Birdman*.

THE GREAT BIRDMAN

RUBICON COMICS GROUP

12¢ 1 MAR

"I'll give you five thousand dollars for that comic book!" yelled a man in the crowd. Everyone turned to look at the man. Then they turned to look at Evan. Evan was quiet for a moment. He faced the man and smiled politely.

"Sorry, but my dad gave this to me, and it's worth more than any amount of money you could offer."

The entire way home, Evan and his dad talked non-stop about their favorite comics. They shared stories they had never told each other before. Neither of them had ever been happier. Especially Evan.

TALK TIP

Reading scripts aloud requires practice and preparation. Rehearse your lines so that you can speak them fluently, naturally, and with the right expression.

SPEAK OUT

With a partner, write a skit for a conversation between Evan and his dad on the way home from the convention. Practice and perform your skit for another pair of students. Evaluate your partner's performance and provide feedback.

STEP 1:
CONSIDER YOUR AUDIENCE

First, think of your readers. Remember, you can't write for everyone. A comic book written for people your age will be very different than one written for your teachers or parents. Narrow down your target audience. What age are your readers? Are they boys or girls? Learn more about your audience before you begin.

TALK TIP

It's important to consider your audience when you are presenting or giving a speech. As you prepare your speaking notes, think of what your audience wants to hear and what will keep them interested.

STEP 2:
DEVELOP AN IDEA

What is your comic about? Consider things your audience might like. Based on your audience's interests, come up with a main story idea. You should also think about what genre you want to write in. There are many genres to choose from, including action, comedy, fantasy, horror, science fiction, and others.

STEP 3:
DEVELOP A STORYLINE

The storyline must keep people interested when they are reading your comic book. Successful comic books have believable characters that connect to a dramatic storyline. This doesn't mean that you must have action and explosions in your story. But do make sure that interesting things happen. Also think of who is going to be in your comic book. How do your characters relate to one another? What happens to them in your story?

STEP 4:
DEVELOP YOUR CHARACTERS

Decide on your characters' names, looks, and personalities. How do they behave? What are their traits? What are their goals, dreams, and fears? Comic-book legend Stan Lee once said that you need a character that people will care about and want to read about. "Mainly, you have to know what his hang-ups are and his problems and his worries, his personal life," he said. "Otherwise he's just a cipher up there."

cipher: person or thing of no importance

TALK TIP

When you repeat what someone else has said, you are quoting him or her. You must give credit and note that you are using another person's words.

STEP 5:
COME UP WITH A TITLE

Remember, the title attracts people to your comic book. It should make people want to open your comic book. Most comic books have titles based on their main characters (for example, *Archie* or *The 99*) or their main story ideas (for example, *Dragon Ball* or *Slam Dunk*).

THE AMAZING HERO GUY

STEP 6:
CREATE A STORYBOARD

A storyboard is a series of drawings that shows what happens in your story. It is like a rough draft of your comic book. Use good paper and a sharpened pencil. Try to keep the pictures simple. Remember to include backgrounds in your drawings. Don't be afraid to make mistakes. You can always redraw as you go along.

STEP 7:
INKING

Once you are happy with your storyboard, trace over your pencil drawings with black ink. Keep the lines clean and crisp. Comic-book drawings should be clear and easy to understand.

STEP 8:
LETTERING

Lettering means writing in the text of your comic book — from captions to dialogue to sound effects. Some people write everything by hand. Others type the words on the computer, print them, and then glue them onto the page.

STEP 9: COLORING

Color your drawings. Keep the colors simple. Colors should be in solid blocks. This means whole areas are colored in the same color. As color adds to the printing costs, many comic books, such as Japanese manga, are simply black and white.

STEP 10: THE FINISHING TOUCH

The very last thing you need is a cover. It should feature your comic book's title and an exciting image to give readers a hint of what's inside. "Give me something I can see from across the room," says Mark Waid, a comic-book editor. "Simple is always, always better." He also suggests bold colors and white space to grab your readers' attention. After you finish your cover, fasten all your pages together and *presto* you've got your very own comic book.

LISTEN UP

When you ask someone a question, listen carefully and patiently to his or her answer. Active listening will help you form good follow-up questions or responses.

SPEAK OUT

Think of a time when you had a creative idea and turned your idea into a reality. Prepare a brief oral narrative telling the story of your experience. Was it hard work? Was it fun? Perform your narrative for a partner, and have your partner evaluate your performance and provide feedback.

Quick Reference

Academic Language

- ○ I agree . . .
- ○ I disagree . . .
- ○ In my opinion . . .
- ○ Excuse me . . .
- ○ I hear what you are saying . . .
- ○ I would like to make clear that . . .
- ○ Thank you for sharing . . .
- ○ What are your thoughts . . .

Partner Reading Techniques

- ○ Follow along as your partner reads.
- ○ Pay attention to your partner.
- ○ Take turns reading in one of the following ways:
    - ✧ Shoulder to shoulder
    - ✧ Chapter by chapter
    - ✧ Frame by frame
    - ✧ Page by page